All the Magic
in the World

by WENDY HARTMANN · *pictures by* NIKI DALY

The Bodley Head · London

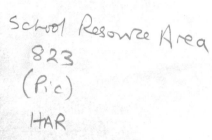

First published in Great Britain 1993 by
The Bodley Head Children's Books
An imprint of Random House UK Ltd
20 Vauxhall Bridge Road,
London SW1V 2SA

Random House Australia (Pty) Limited
20 Alfred Street,
Milsons Point, Sydney,
New South Wales 2061, Australia

Random House New Zealand Limited
18 Poland Road, Glenfield,
Auckland 10, New Zealand

Random House South Africa (Pty) Ltd
PO Box 337, Bergvlei 2012, South Africa

Typeset in the USA
Printed and bound in Hong Kong

A catalogue record for this book is available
from the British Library

ISBN 0 370 31788 2

For my father
WH

For my mother
ND

Every Friday evening, Sonnie, Stefan, Anna, Chrissie, and Lena played in the street or in the yard.

If it had rained, they made mud socks on their feet and paraded past the chickens, making silly noises.

If it was cold, they crowded around the roadworker's drum to watch the orange flames lick at the damp air. Firelight painted them gold and warm. Sometimes they talked about Joseph, the odd-job man. Joseph always had a tin.

'For my special things,' he told them.

But they laughed. 'Silly old Joseph,' they whispered, 'picking up junk to keep in a tin.'

One evening, Sonnie, Stefan, and Chrissie climbed the milk-
wood tree to hang like monkeys in the branches, and Anna drew
pictures in the sand. But Lena stood at the gate.

Lena who was teased because she stumbled on stairs
and fell out of trees. Little Lena who always tripped over her own feet.
She twanged out music with a piece of broken wire, pulling it
back and letting it go so that it hit the metal sign.

She turned towards Joseph. He sat alone at the corner of his shop with his tin on his lap. Lena crept closer. He smiled at her.

'It's my special tin,' he said. 'There's nothing in it to spend or to eat. But...' And she sat down to listen. Out of the tin he pulled an old piece of string. It was twisted and full of knots.

'This was around a package,' he said, 'and then it was thrown away.' He carefully undid all the knots and tied the two ends of the string together. 'But look, it can make pictures.'

'A cup and saucer,' said Lena.

'A house.... Magic!'

The others ran to see. Joseph took Lena's hand. In it he placed a shell, pearly white and smooth. Its empty insides held the sound of the sea. They heard it whisper when they pressed the shell close to their ears. And when they shut their eyes tight, they could almost smell the salt on the waves.

Then Joseph shook the tin. It made a mysterious sound. 'Look,' he said, emptying a fistful of pull-tops on to the ground. Rings gleamed in the evening light and shiny tongues curled on the sand.

He sent Anna for a piece of flat wood and Sonnie for a smooth round stone. Then he hammered and bent and hammered and bent, all the while telling his story. 'I was lucky to find these.' He winked at Lena. 'You know, when they are all put together, they become a magic chain. And anyone who wears it'–he bent the last link –'becomes a princess.'

Joseph got up and stood in front of Lena. He put the silver chain around her neck and bowed low.

'Your Highness,' he said.

Her Royal Highness Princess Lena curtsied. She smiled a princess's smile and walked around Stefan and Chrissie, her arms outstretched, her head held high. The silver chain glittered around her neck and everyone saw how graceful she was.

She danced a little dance like the wind across the wheat fields.

'You have magic in that tin,' she whispered.

'No, Lena,' said Joseph. 'There is no magic in my tin. All the magic in the world is not found in tins.'

'Where is it found, then?' the children asked.

Joseph smiled. 'You've seen the things - things I pick up here and there.' They nodded.

'You saw the shell?'

'Yes,' they said, 'we heard the sea.'

'You saw the pull-tops?'

'Yes.'

'And you *saw* the princess.'

Joseph shut the tin.

'So you tell me where the magic is found.'